THE WUMPLES OF WIGWUMP

by Peggy C. Clarke

Pictures by Jennifer Hicks

Cuchullain Publications

Fort Wayne, Indiana

Cuchullain Publications
P.O. Box 10941
Fort Wayne, IN 46854-0941

First Edition. Library of Congress in Publication Data:
Clarke, Margaret C., The Wumples of WigWump
by Margaret C. Clarke. Summary: Fanciful Monster-
types discover happiness through a bird's song.
ISBN 0-9614659-8-0 (1. Monsters-Fiction. 2. Happiness Fiction)

Illustrated by: Jennifer Hicks

Published by: Cuchullain Publications
Fort Wayne, Indiana

To my parents, Casey and Vivian,
for my wonderful childhood.
Thank you for your love and support.

WigWump is a land that is far, far away.
To travel there takes fifteen nights and one day.
The Wumples who live there are unusual creatures.
They're related to monsters and have few charming features.
Now don't pack your bags. You won't want to visit.
WigWump's not a kingdom to visit...OR IS IT?

WIGWUMP
15 NIGHTS
AND 1 DAY

Wumples, in general, are an unhappy group.
They eat only weeds, which make terrible soup.

WEED ON A STICK 5¢
WEED CREAM CONE 12¢
CREAM OF CRABGRASS

No ice cream or cupcakes or anything sweet;
Just tall weeds and short weeds. That's all Wumples eat.

They don't go to parties or play in the park.
In fact, if they could, they'd stay in until dark.

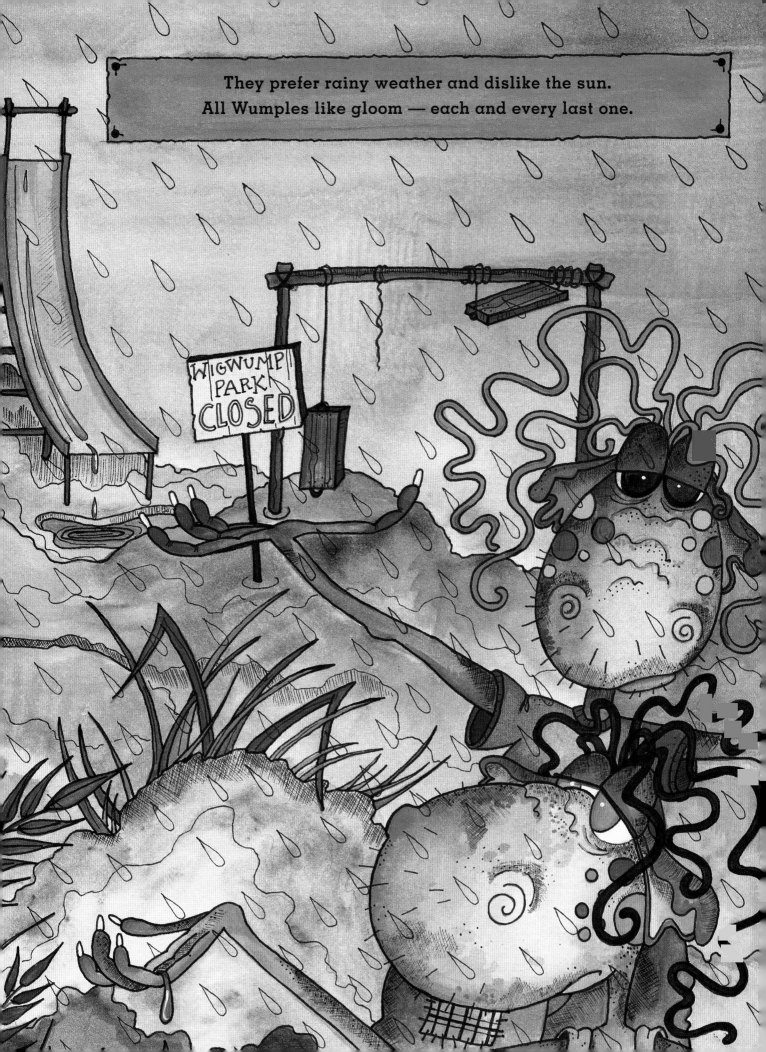

They prefer rainy weather and dislike the sun.
All Wumples like gloom — each and every last one.

Wumples get little sleep, which keeps them
quite grumpy.
Could you get much sleep if your bed was
all lumpy?
Their tables and chairs are all made
out of rock.
You won't find a painting, a rug,
or a clock.

Young Wumples learn fast not to play
in the yard.
Who wants to play in a yard
that's so hard?
The rocks skin their knees and destroy
all their toys.
It's no fun at all for the
girls or the boys.

WigWump is not pretty. Believe me, it's true.
You won't find a flower in red, pink, or blue.
The Wumples don't speak when they pass on the street.
They never look up. They just look at their feet.

Now don't get me wrong, the Wumples aren't mean.
They're just the unhappiest group you've ever seen.
Could anything happen to change this routine?
Something did happen! It happened this Spring!

A storm hit a kingdom five kingdoms away.
A poor little bird blew off course that dark day.

He flew through the night. The bird flew a long way.
He needed to rest. In WigWump he would stay.

The next day a Wumple walked
by the bird's tree.
He noticed some movement and
stretched up to see.
This new little creature looked tired
and weak.
So he dug in his weeds and left seeds
by his beak.

The next day the Wumple walked
back to the tree.
He heard a strange noise, but what could
this noise be?
He had never heard music.
He had never heard song.
It did not sound gloomy, but it
did not sound wrong.

The next thing he knew, something changed on his face.
Where there had been a frown, was a smile in it's place.
He went back to WigWump and the Wumples all came.
Then they studied his face for this grin had no name.
What had just happened? They all came to see.
Why, he actually looked happy, so they went to this tree.

The bird wished to greet them. They gathered around.
Then — there! — they all heard it, the most wonderful sound!
It made them feel happy. It made them feel bright.
What used to feel wrong, began to feel right.

Some tried hard to whistle and some
sang out loud.
These noises made music, which made
them feel proud.
The Wumples agreed that this feeling
must stay.
They'd all work to keep this good feeling
each day.

They went back to their homes to plant flowers and grass.
They hung bright colored curtains on windows of glass.

WIGWUMP PARK OPEN

CREAM OF BUBBLE GUM SOUP
OOEY GOOEY
STICKY CHEWY
CHOCOLAT
DANDY CANDY APPLE ...

The children went outside to play with their toys.
WigWump was now filled with this wonderful noise.

Now when the Wumples walk by
on the street,
They bow and they curtsy
whenever they meet.
They grin a big grin, asking,
"How do you do?"
Away walk the Wumples, all smiles,
two by two.

One boy learned to smile. It spread very fast.
WigWump's now a happy place. Finally! At last!
So now when you hear that great magical sound,
Remember one bird turned a town all around.
Now pack your bags if you're planning to visit.
WigWump's now a kingdom to visit...OR IS IT?

**WIGWUMP
15 NIGHTS
AND 1 DAY**

Coming Soon From the Wumples of WigWump Series

Written by Peggy C. Clarke

WIGWUMP'S WACKY WEATHER
A WILD WACKIT IN WIGWUMP
WUMPLES AND WEEBLOBS
A WUMPLE'S NEW SCHOOL